FRANKENSTEIN

MARY SHELLEY

D0062076

FRANKENSTEIN

MARY SHELLEY

www.realreads.co.uk

Retold by Gill Tavner
Illustrated by Vanessa Lubach

Published by Real Reads Ltd
Stroud, Gloucestershire, UK
www.realreads.co.uk

Text copyright © Gill Tavner 2008
Illustrations copyright © Vanessa Lubach 2008
The right of Gill Tavner to be identified as author of
this book has been asserted by her in accordance with the
Copyright, Design and Patents Act 1988

First published in 2008
Reprinted 2010, 2011

All rights reserved
No part of this publication may be reproduced or transmitted in any
form or by any means, electronic or mechanical, including
photocopy, recording, or any information storage and retrieval
system, without permission in writing from the publisher.

ISBN 978-1-906230-17-3

Printed in China by Wai Man Book Binding (China) Ltd
Designed by Lucy Guenot
Typeset by Bookcraft Ltd, Stroud, Gloucestershire

CONTENTS

THE CHARACTERS

Robert Walton

Walton is the captain of a boat trapped by ice in the frozen north. Who is the man he pulls from the sea? Can he save him?

Victor Frankenstein

After years of study, Victor creates a living creature. Why does he flee from his creation? Can he keep his family safe? Will he help the monster or will they pursue each other until death?

Elizabeth Lavenza

Victor's adopted sister and future bride. Can Victor keep her safe?

Henry Clerval

Clerval has been Victor's
friend since childhood.
Can he help Victor? Can he
escape the monster's fury?

The Monster

The monster has been rejected by
his creator and by all of mankind.
Can he persuade Victor to help
him, or will his fury lead to further
violence? Who is stronger, the monster or
his creator? Who is more to blame?

Justine Moritz

Justine has been a loyal maid to
the Frankenstein family for many
years. Will her innocence keep her
safe from the curse upon them?

FRANKENSTEIN

To Mrs Saville,
England
August 13th, 1721

My dearest sister,

Since my last letter, my long voyage has been interrupted by an event that has thrilled my heart with expectation, chilled my soul with terror, and ignited my mind with the most violent imaginings.

As you know, I set out on this dangerous journey across the icy seas to the North Pole in a quest to discover more about the mysteries of the ocean. My desire is to find a route which will further mankind's understanding of our natural world.

The voyage has been long, my dear sister, and is not yet over. I have felt bitter loneliness, in spite of my crew. We are, I believe, but half a person when we lack a similar soul with whom we can share our heart's deepest concerns. I have been such a half-person for many months. Dear sister, please share my joy when I tell you that the sympathetic ocean has delivered me the companion I need.

Two days before we found my new friend, a bewildering scene passed before my eyes. Trapped by ice, I looked from our stranded vessel over the land of frost, and saw a sledge, pulled by dogs, carrying a being the shape of a man. He was, however, of such a gigantic stature that I must call him a monster rather than a man. As I stared, his dogs pulled his sledge away beyond my sight.

I tell you this tale because it is strangely connected with my friend. Two days later, I heard my crew shouting and rushing to one side of the boat. They pulled a man, half-dead with cold, from a broken island of ice. We dried and warmed him and fed him soup which restored him wonderfully, but he remains weak.

Over the last week, I have formed a strong friendship with our slowly recovering guest. His name is Victor Frankenstein. Although his eyes have a wild expression, a gentle smile lights his face when he receives a kindness. Most of the time, however, his deep grief fills me with sympathy and compassion. Dear sister, he is the companion I have so long lacked, for he speaks the language of my heart and of my deeper imagination, an imagination which is now deeply troubled by the tale he has told me.

When I shared with Frankenstein the reasons for my journey, he experienced great violence of feeling. 'Unhappy man,' he groaned, 'do you share my madness and ambition?' He beat his fists against his forehead and his body trembled. 'Walton, you must hear my tale. You must hear my terrible, terrible tale so that you do not follow

my journey to hell.' He leaned forward, his eyes wild, his cold hand gripping my arm. 'I have attempted what no man should attempt. I have pushed the boundaries of the natural world and they can never be restored.'

I sat, entranced and terrified.

What follows here, dear sister, is Victor Frankenstein's story, and that of the monster he created. It will fill you with terror to learn of the horrors my friend has endured. I tremble as I record his words.

Your affectionate brother,
Robert Walton.

VICTOR FRANKENSTEIN'S STORY

Like you, Walton, I wanted to increase my understanding of life and the world. Let my story be a warning to you.

A human being is a powerful creation. We continually stretch the boundaries of our knowledge and our power. We can cure, heal and kill. I used to wonder whether it might be possible to defeat death. Could it be within our power to relight a spark of life in a dead body? Could we, by deep study of darker powers, become god-like creators of a new living being? And, if we could break the laws of nature in this way, what would we create? Would it be a gentle creature of love, or a monster?

The laws of nature governed my childhood. Living in the dramatically beautiful Swiss Alps, I spent idyllic years within a happy family. Although I loved my two younger brothers dearly, I spent most of my time with my adopted sister, Elizabeth.

A harmony between our young souls formed the basis of our affection. I felt great pride and delight in Elizabeth's loving nature, her golden hair and her blue eyes so full of sensitivity and sweetness. We complemented each other's characters perfectly, achieving together a balance between my passionate curiosity about the world, and Elizabeth's simple enjoyment of its beauty. Our energetic, adventurous playmate, Henry Clerval, added a liveliness to the mix without which we would not have been complete. Three souls in perfect harmony.

By the time I reached the age of seventeen, it was clear that my extreme hunger for knowledge would lead me away. Our family's first separation came when I left to study at Ingolstadt University.

'You must write frequently,' said my father. 'If you fail to write I shall know that you are displeased with yourself; that your pursuits are not admirable.'

'I will write regularly, I promise,' I whispered tenderly to Elizabeth as I held her sobbing breast close to my own. 'When I come back, we shall become more than friends – far, far more.' I kissed her tearful eyes before climbing into my carriage and beginning my fateful journey.

Universities are full of inspiring thinkers and great minds. I was introduced to new areas of knowledge and challenged by the excitement of ideas.

'I will explore unknown powers,' I wrote enthusiastically to Elizabeth, 'I will discover the deepest mysteries of creation. Perhaps with more study, I will break through the boundary between life and death. Perhaps I am destined to reverse the natural process by which we all die. Maybe I can defeat death.'

My desire to discover the very core of human existence quickly became an obsession. Could I – I wondered – could I possibly create a human life? The thought chilled me to the core, but thrilled me more.

To understand life, I first had to understand death. Day after day, night after night, I worked alone in tombs, in mortuaries, in graveyards and in slaughterhouses. Decaying bodies, robbed of their former beauty, their eyes and

brains now inherited by worms, became my only companions. The world of Victor Frankenstein became a dark one – a world of dark places and darker forces.

Cold and alone, I walked amongst the dead. One dark and dreadful night, I made the fateful decision to try to create a being of my own. Alone in dark, dreary, misty graveyards, alone in echoing tombs and mortuaries, I gathered the human remains I would need – limbs, organs, nerves, veins, a brain. These I carried, under the cover of darkness, to my attic room, where I began the terrible process of assembling a human body.

A letter arrived from my father. 'My dear Victor,' he wrote, 'we have not heard from you for many months. We are all well, but we fear for you. How are you spending your time?'

I did not reply.

How could I possibly tell my father that I spent my time alone, in dim candlelight, working on all the fine details of a human body? How could I explain that I hadn't seen daylight for many months? How could I express my increasing belief that I would soon become the god-like creator of a new species? Worse still, if I could explain, what would my father say?

The months passed and the lifeless body neared completion. As I grew closer to creating life, my own neglected body developed an ever-closer resemblance to death. Increasingly thin and pale, I was unable to sleep, unable to laugh. My eyes, strained by the intricate work of fusing together nerves and veins, became wild and bloodshot. As November drew to its dismal close, my stomach constantly churned with anxiety and, although I failed to recognise it at the time, with guilt.

One violently stormy November night, the completed lifeless thing lay before me, with cables attached. The room was cold and dark. It was close to midnight. Impatiently awaiting the next flash of lightning, I trembled with excitement and dread. For a while, the storm seemed to calm. The room was silent and still.

I waited.

The thing on the floor waited too.

The flash, when it came, was sudden, but I was ready. As the room flared with god-given light, I transferred its energy to my own creation.

I held my breath and watched.

Nothing happened.

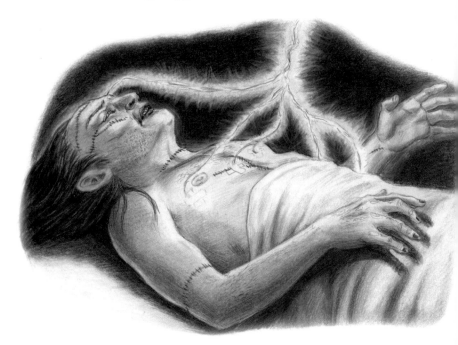

Then slowly a dull, yellow eye opened;
the creature breathed hard with foul-smelling
breath. Its arms and legs jerked awkwardly.
I was horrified. My dream exploded around
me. I had created life, but never had I seen
anything so frightening, so unnatural and so
ugly. I fled from my creation in horror and
disgust, slamming the door behind me.

Hours later, I paced my bedroom. What
had I done? What should I do now? How could
this possibly end well? Exhausted, I fell into a
troubled sleep. For the first time since I had
left I dreamed of my family, but my dream
was far from comforting. I dreamed I held
Elizabeth in my arms and kissed her tenderly,
but as we kissed I realised that her lips were
cold, her body lifeless. She was dead.

Horrified and sweating, I woke with a
start. The being I had created, the monster,
had entered my room. Its pale yellow eyes
were fixed on me. In a vain attempt to speak,

it slowly opened its jaw. The sight was terrible.
The sounds were terrible. The smell was
terrible. The monster's face contorted and
what looked like a grin wrinkled its cheek. It
slowly reached out an arm in a clumsy attempt
to touch my face. Screaming, I leapt from my
bed and fled the room.

The monster, abandoned by me, its creator, for the second time in the few short hours of its life, watched me go.

Afraid to return to my apartment, I hid from my demonic creation in the courtyard. As rain fell upon me from the black and comfortless sky, I trembled for hours with cold and terror. Gradually, the pale light of dawn made the world less hostile. I watched a coach appear and saw a man descend and pay the coachman. I recognised the man. Suddenly, my horror was replaced by joyful relief. It was my childhood friend. 'Henry!' I cried out, 'How glad I am to see you!'

'My dear Victor, I have just arrived in Ingolstadt. How strange that we should meet immediately. Why are you out in this rain? We have all been so worried about you, and rightly so. You are terribly thin and pale. Are you ill?'

I led Clerval towards my rooms. He waited below whilst I went upstairs. I held my breath as I opened the bedroom door. Would the hideous wretch be waiting for me? The room was empty. Almost faint with relief, I called for Clerval to join me. I laughed, a loud, unrestrained laugh. My wild eyes frightened him. 'Oh Henry, save me!' I cried, as I collapsed at my friend's feet.

I was dangerously ill. Clerval nursed me with devoted attention through the dark winter months. As spring approached and my strength began to return, Clerval began to talk to me about home.

Oh, the beautiful scenes he brought to mind: our home on the shores of Lake Geneva, the greenery of the spring and the majesty of the mountains. We talked about my beautiful Elizabeth from whom I had now been absent for five years. Clerval described the golden curls and laughing blue eyes of my darling youngest brother William, rosy with health. I even began to miss our gentle, pretty maid, Justine Moritz, who had been with our

family since our shared childhood. And my father, my dear, dignified father to whom I had given five years of unease. How my selfish pursuits had locked away my love for them all! I longed to return.

'They cannot see me this weak,' I told Clerval. 'I will write to tell them that I am well and that I shall return soon.'

I had wasted months of Clerval's time. He was now keen to study oriental literature and languages. Anxious to avoid my previous interests, I joined him. This study gave me pleasure: unlike the heroic poetry of Greece and Rome, oriental writers told of warm sun and human passions. Clerval and I shared our study and our leisure. Our summer walks in the mountains restored my strength and my senses. One thing I was too afraid to share with him, however, was my terrible secret.

Winter returned to Ingolstadt. I resolved to return home the following spring. Oh that I had not so selfishly delayed! When May arrived, we were still absorbed in our studies. A letter from my father changed everything.

Dear Victor,
You must return. Instead of the cheerful home you would have found a month ago, you will find only tears and wretchedness.

William is dead! Worse than dead, our beautiful boy is murdered. He went out to play and did not return. After searching all night, I found his poor little body, dark finger marks of strangulation on his throat. A small pendant he was wearing was stolen and must have been the motive. How can there be evil dark enough to destroy such radiant innocence? Come home, Victor, and bring us love and healing.

Your loving father.

Leaving Clerval to settle my affairs, I began the journey home. The route was beautiful, but my heart was heavy. After a few days, I found myself looking down upon beautiful Lake Geneva for the first time in six years. 'Dear mountains!' I called, 'Does your beauty predict future peace or mock our unhappiness?' That night, the mountains answered in such a way that I foresaw my destiny. That night I learned that I was to be the most wretched of human beings.

I had sought shelter from a sudden violent storm. As I watched in awe, one flash of lightning, brighter than the others, illuminated before me a gigantic, deformed figure. The lightning also illuminated my mind – surely no human could have killed my beautiful brother. I had created my brother's murderer. The monster I had created two years before disappeared into the darkness.

My happy home was being torn apart by even worse sorrow than I had expected. 'Justine is accused of the murder,' sobbed Elizabeth as I held her in my arms.

'They are mistaken!' I exclaimed. 'I know the murderer.' I knew that it wasn't our loyal Justine. My precious Elizabeth looked at me with fearful sympathy. 'You have been ill,' she soothed. 'This shock is too great.'

I knew then that nobody would believe my story. I could not share my knowledge.

'The missing necklace was found in Justine's pocket,' explained Elizabeth. 'She will be tried tomorrow. Oh Victor, I believe entirely in her innocence.'

Poor, innocent Justine Moritz calmly faced her trial. 'God knows my innocence,' she said softly, but she was unable to explain how the necklace had been found in her possession. 'I have no enemy who would want to destroy me by placing the stolen necklace in my pocket.'

I had full faith in the justice of our land.
Darling Elizabeth spoke passionately in
defence of Justine's character, describing her
as the gentlest, most loving of creatures. I felt
therefore the full horror of shock when Justine
was condemned to die. I gnashed my teeth and
groaned in bitter agony. I carried hell within me.

William and Justine were the first two
innocent victims of my unhallowed arts. The
next day, I looked at my heart-broken family.
'You will have more grief and more funerals,' I
said inwardly. 'These are not your last tears.'

I had only ever wanted to serve mankind.
Instead, I had created murderous destruction.
For weeks I suffered deep despair and was
unable to offer comfort to my family. Often, I
was tempted to plunge into the waters of the lake
and end my tortures forever. I knew, however,
that I had to protect my family from the fiend's
malice. I lived only that I might kill the monster.

Two months had passed since Justine's cruel death. During my waking hours I suffered a heavy melancholy. Sleep alone brought me comfort and only sleep's dreams could bring me joy. Seeking greater relief, I decided to travel alone towards the majestic mountains around Chamonix.

Travelling first by horse and then by donkey I progressed deeper into the mountains. Their awesome grandeur, and the sound of the river raging against the rocks, reminded me of powers both greater and more permanent than my own – this, and the gentle breeze, soothed me. When I finally arrived in Chamonix I gazed in wonder at the eternal beauty of the snow-capped mountains and immense glaciers. I resolved the next morning to climb to the summit of Montanvert, in the shadow of Mont Blanc's awful majesty.

The ascent was precipitous. By midday I had gained great height. Two hours later, having traversed the glacier, I rested upon a rock and gazed at Montanvert's summit. The sight gave wings to my soul and my heart swelled with something like joy. Oh that such a sensation could last! Alas, that was not to be.

At some distance, I beheld the figure of a man, bounding over crevices towards me at superhuman speed. A faintness seized me as his hideous form grew nearer and more distinct. Trembling with rage and horror, I leapt to my feet as he approached. 'Devil!' I cried, 'Vile murderer!'

The monster looked down upon me with a mixture of malice and bitter agony. 'You are my creator, yet you wish me dead. How dare you play with life? I have known misery beyond that of all living things. I beg you to listen to me.'

'Detestable fiend!' I leapt upon him, but he easily eluded me.

'Be calm. Listen to me and do your duty towards me or I will spill the blood of all your remaining friends.'

'Abhorred monster! Cursed be the day on which I gave you life.'

'Why do you seek to increase my misery? I, your own creature, would be obedient to you, my natural lord and king. My soul once glowed with love, but I was spurned by everybody. Everywhere I see happiness from which I am excluded. Misery has made me a fiend. Make me happy and I shall be virtuous. If you fail me, you, your family and thousands of others will be swallowed up in the whirlwinds of my rage.'

Feeling fear, curiosity and some dawning compassion, and beginning to realise that I had responsibilities towards my creation, I followed him to a hut high on the mountainside, where he began his tale.

THE MONSTER'S STORY

When I was first spurned by you, my creator, I fled to a forest. I was cold and hungry. My eyes did not yet see clearly, and I understood little of my surroundings. Entirely alone, I sat and wept. That night, I found a place where some people had recently been. I found a cloak to cover my naked body. They had left a warm fire.

I learned to feed it constantly with wood, and was afraid to leave it throughout that cold, lonely winter. As my senses gradually developed, I became aware of the moon in the sky marking the passage of time. Its peaceful beauty gave me comfort. I watched the creatures of the forest, learning from them to eat berries and nuts and to drink the clear waters of the streams.

When the spring sun began to warm the earth, I tore myself away from my fire and travelled in search of friends. I approached a small village, hoping for welcome, but the villagers screamed and threw stones at me. I was terrified, and ran away until I found a small woodshed. I settled there, pleased to find shelter from the weather and mankind's barbarity.

In the cottage adjoining my shelter lived a blind old man with his son and daughter. I was able to watch them closely through a dusty window in the wall separating our homes. They worked hard all day. The son chopped wood and his sister worked the land. There seemed to be much affection between the three, and the children cared for their blind father with great benevolence.

I resolved to help them with their hard labours. Knowing too well the reaction of mankind towards me, I could only leave my shed under cover of darkness. At night I chopped wood and piled logs at their door. In the cold months I cleared snow from their path. They were filled with wonder, and talked of a 'good spirit' sent to help them.

Early on I had noticed that they made sounds to each other, which could bring a smile or a frown. What a god-like science! I resolved to study their sounds closely and learn, if I could, to talk like them. Over several months I listened to them carefully, practising the sounds alone when they slept. I grew to love this family, admiring their gentleness towards each other, and their beauty. How I longed to be with them!

I yearned for their sweet smiles to be directed towards me.

I decided that I would not approach them until I had mastered language. I had some hope then that they might see my gentle soul, rather than my ugliness. Alas, whenever I beheld my reflection in a stream I felt only despair and horror. Who was I? What was I? Why had my creator made me so hideous and then turned from me in disgust? In the bitterness of my heart I cursed you, Victor Frankenstein.

After months of careful study, I felt ready to test my fate. On that day's success depended all of my future happiness. I planned to go in when the blind man was alone. Unable to see my ugliness, he might feel enough goodwill towards me to mediate between me and his children. Almost faint with terror, I knocked upon his door.

'Kind sir, I am a traveller in want of a little rest,' I began. He let me in and offered me food. Somewhat encouraged, I continued. 'I am an unfortunate creature travelling towards some dear friends who have never seen me. I fear that they may be blinded by a fatal prejudice, and receive me only as a detestable monster rather than the loving and generous friend I truly am.'

'You sound gentle and sincere,' answered the blind man. 'I am sure that your friends will show you brotherly love.'

I sobbed at his words and fell to my knees. 'Oh, these are the first words of kindness ever directed towards me. How grateful I am to you.' At that moment I heard footsteps

approaching the house. His children had returned earlier than expected. 'Save me!' I cried, grabbing the old man's hand. 'You and your family are the friends I seek. Protect me!'

The rest is chaos. I remember shrieks of 'Fiend!' as the son attacked me. The daughter fainted, and the trembling father cried 'Good god, what are you?' I could have killed them all, but my despair weakened me. I crawled back to my shelter and the next day I left, carrying hell within me. Filled with rage and sorrow, I declared war upon all of mankind, but mostly upon you, my heartless creator.

Throughout that winter I travelled across the hard earth in an uncertain direction. The cold and hardship, which would have killed a lesser being, strengthened my spirit of revenge. By the time I reached Geneva, my hellish rage had been further inflamed by suffering.

Tired and hungry, I sat beside the lake. As I sat, a boy appeared. His blonde curly hair gave him the appearance of an angel. Softened a little by my present weakness, I foolishly hoped he might accept and befriend me. Alas, he screamed when he saw me. In confused disappointment, I grabbed him and held him tightly.

'Ugly monster! Let me go! My father Alphonse Frankenstein will punish you.'

Frankenstein! My enemy was not invulnerable. I had been presented with the means of hurting you. Your brother's struggle was brief. As he died I felt hellish triumph.

I took from his neck a small pendant and sought shelter in a nearby barn. In the barn I found a girl peacefully asleep. She smiled as she dreamed. Angry that no beautiful girl would ever smile at me, I placed the pendant in her pocket. Imagine the satisfaction I felt when I learned that this small action was to cause you further suffering.

Now I am alone and miserable. I yearn for a companion, but no human will associate with me. You must create for me another being of my species. As two monsters we will have affection between us. We will find a deserted corner of the earth and never trouble mankind again.

I see compassion in your eyes. Do you swear to help me? Good. I will leave you now, but I shall always be near you. When my mate is ready, I shall appear.

VICTOR FRANKENSTEIN'S STORY CONTINUED

During the monster's story, my feelings towards him had softened. However, his description of William's murder and his encounter with Justine revived my horror and rage. I agreed to his demands in a wild confusion of feelings. He was a sensitive soul and there was justice in his argument. Did not I, his creator, have a responsibility to make him happy? Alas, what might be the consequences for mankind if I were to create another such fiend? If I failed, what might be the consequences for my family?

I returned home, responsibility weighing upon me with a mountain's weight. My poor father, anxious to relieve my distress, suggested that my long-expected wedding to Elizabeth might help to lift my melancholy.

'Father, I love Elizabeth tenderly and sincerely. Marriage to her would bring me happiness beyond my deserts. First, however, I have a task I must perform. I must travel to England for further study, but every day of my absence I shall long for the day when I might be united with my darling Elizabeth.'

English philosophers had recently made great discoveries that would be valuable to me in my task. I needed to talk with them. When Henry heard that I was to travel to England he was keen to accompany me, and I was pleased to have such a pleasant companion.

Dear Clerval! Beloved friend! Even now it delights me to remember your wild enthusiasm for every new scene upon that journey. Is that all that remains of you? Memories?

It was October when we arrived in London. I began to collect the materials and knowledge I would need for my new creation. It was a terrible process, and I felt constant unease about my undertaking.

Keeping my activities a secret from Clerval became increasingly difficult. In March I decided to travel alone to an island in Orkney, where I could work without human contact. Clerval would travel around Scotland, meeting me in Perth at a time when I thought my dread task might be completed.

The isles of Orkney offered me everything I needed. Far from the attention of my fellow humans, I worked day and night with grim determination upon my second ghastly creation. In the evenings I stood on the cliff tops, and found relief in the desolate wildness of the sea.

As the monster's mate neared completion, my misgivings increased. What if she was ten thousand times more evil than he? Rather than fulfilling his promise, she might terrorise mankind with fiendish hatred.

With fear filling my mind, I looked up from my intricate work. By the light of the moon I saw the demon at my window, a ghastly grin

wrinkling his lips. He looked with delight upon his future mate. A terrible thought chilled my heart. What if they were to produce children? Was I right to inflict this curse upon future generations?

Was it possible that, in saving my family, I was threatening the future of mankind? The wickedness of my work suddenly burst upon me.

Trembling with passion, I tore the body I was creating to pieces. Seeing me destroy the mate upon whom he depended for his future happiness, the wretch at the window howled with despair and fury. Minutes later, he burst in through my doorway.

'Do you dare to break your promise?' He struggled to control his sorrow and anger. 'Do you dare to destroy my hopes?'

'I cannot create another demon to terrorise mankind.'

'Fool! Have you understood nothing? You are to marry soon. Are you to be happy whilst I am wretched? No! I am fearless, and therefore powerful. I will make you more miserable than you can imagine.'

'I cannot do for you what you demand.'

'Then be warned. I will be with you on your wedding night.'

I was alone, separated from everyone I loved.
The monster's warning made it clear to me that
I was to be his next victim, and that my wedding
night was his chosen time. I would not fear him.
I would be prepared for a bitter struggle.

I was to meet Clerval in Perth in two days'
time. Before then, I had to dispose of the
mangled remains of my half-finished creature.
Shuddering with disgust, I put them into a
sack along with many stones. That night I put
out to sea in a small boat and, when the moon
hid behind a cloud, I threw my dreadful load
overboard. The sack gurgled as it sank.

With a new sense of calm, I rowed back to land. I could not have foreseen the calamity that awaited me.

The desolate beach I had left was now a scene of some excitement. A small crowd had gathered by the water's edge. As I struck ground, men ran to me and roughly pulled me from my boat.

'Is this he?' asked an angry voice.

A woman looked at me. 'No,' she answered, 'the man who rowed away was much bigger, almost a giant.'

At her words, my stomach tightened. The moon cast eerie shadows on the crowd, and for the first time I noticed in their centre the body of a man lying lifeless on the ground. I walked towards it. I still shudder with the same agony when I remember seeing the corpse with black finger marks of strangulation upon his neck. I threw myself down upon the body in grief. It was still warm. 'Oh Henry,' I cried, 'are you, too, deprived of life? Why did you seek me here? Why didn't you wait in Perth?'

The shock was too great for me. The villagers took me indoors, and I spent the next two months on the point of death. Oh, had I died then the monster's work would have been complete. Alas, I was doomed to live.

I needed to return to Geneva to protect my family. Elizabeth greeted me with concern. 'Dear Victor, how much you have suffered! I love you, but will be miserable in our marriage if I cannot make you happy.'

I assured her that any hope I had for future happiness lay in her alone. My father, eager to move beyond our recent horrors, urged us to marry soon. We readily agreed. I now knew that within a few short weeks I would know my fate. The monster's words haunted me: 'I will be with you on your wedding night.'

Our wedding on the shore of Lake Geneva was serenely beautiful. United at last to my darling Elizabeth I felt a new contentment, perhaps even optimism. However, the evening sky threatened a storm as we sailed over the lake to the opposite shore for our first night together. My spirits darkening with the sky, I became anxious and watchful.

Elizabeth noticed that I was carrying a pistol. 'What do you fear?'

'This night is one of dread,' I answered. 'When it is passed, all will be safe.' I explained that this night only we should sleep apart, for I did not want her to be distressed by the night's events. 'Tomorrow I will tell you all.'

Leaving Elizabeth in her chamber, her sweet kiss lingering on my lips, I searched the house for my enemy. My foolish search was interrupted by a shrill scream. It was Elizabeth. The awful truth instantly dawned upon me. Elizabeth screamed again, and I rushed to her room.

How did I not die the very moment I saw my wife's lifeless body thrown across the bed? Her head was hanging down, her beautiful features half hidden by her golden hair. The fiend's murderous fingerprints were on her neck.

A movement at the window caught my eye. I looked up to see the hideous monster. He pointed towards his latest victim and laughed. 'I am satisfied,' he jeered. I fired my pistol, but the fiend escaped. Oh, why had I misunderstood his warning? I cursed him and devoted myself to his destruction.

I have pursued the fiend relentlessly across the Mediterranean, the Black Sea and Russia, and into the frozen north. Like him, I carry hell within me. I am motivated by my furious desire for revenge, but I am weak now. I dread dying before I can fulfil my task. Swear to me, Walton, that he shall not escape. Swear that you will destroy my terrible creation.

What dangers did I fail to foresee when I combined my vivid imagination with my powers of analysis and hard work? Oh Walton, when the fiend is dead, avoid all ambition and seek only the happiness offered by love and tranquillity.

August 26th, 1721

My dear sister,
Having told his tale, Victor Frankenstein weakened. As he died, he called out to his beloved dead, 'I move towards you now. My task will be completed by another.'

Oh sister, how can I describe my distress at the death of such a glorious spirit? I covered his body and sought the comfort of the icy winds on deck.

As I returned to him, I heard a horrific howl of grief and horror, 'Oh my creator, I cannot ask your pardon.' I ran to the cabin, and cannot describe the distorted figure I found there, weeping over the body. My first instinct was to fulfil my promise and kill him, but his wretchedness made me pause.

'Fiend, how can you weep with remorse now that your work is done?'

'I no longer seek sympathy or understanding,' responded the monster. 'I have learned to suffer alone, but do you not see that my suffering has been greater than his? I sought love, but found only cruel hatred. Am I truly worse than mankind?

Driven by fury, I killed, but I was broken-hearted each time. Now, my own is the only death I seek. Death will be the first comfort I have ever known. I shall leave you now and travel to the earth's most northern point, where I shall build my funeral pyre. I will ascend it with triumph, and exalt in the agony of the flames. Farewell. May you find safe passage home.'

He leapt from the cabin window and onto his ice raft, and was soon borne away into the darkness from whence he had come.

TAKING THINGS FURTHER

The real read

This *Real Read* version of *Frankenstein* is a retelling of Mary Shelley's magnificent work. If you would like to read the full novel in all its original splendour, many complete editions are available, from bargain paperbacks to beautifully-bound hardbacks. You should be able to find a copy in your local library.

Filling in the spaces

The loss of so many of Mary Shelley's original words is a sad but necessary part of the shortening process. We have had to make some difficult decisions, omitting subplots and details, some important, some less so, but all interesting. We have also, at times, taken the liberty of combining two events into one, or of giving a character words or actions that originally belong to another. The points below will fill in some of the gaps, but nothing can beat the original.

- Victor Frankenstein's two brothers, William and Ernest, play a larger part in the original story than they do here.

- Elizabeth has been adopted from a very poor family.

- Victor's mother dies of scarlet fever just before he first goes to university. Her dying wish is that Victor and Elizabeth should marry.

- Elizabeth feels somewhat responsible for William's murder, as she allowed him to wear the pendant which she believes provided the murderer's motive.

- The monster finds Justine asleep in a barn in which she was seeking shelter while searching for William.

- The family watched by the monster are a French family called the de Laceys. They receive a Turkish visitor, a girl called Safie. As they teach Safie their language, the monster listens carefully. This makes his acquisition of language more credible.

- The de Laceys are now living in exile from France, where Felix de Lacey helped Safie and her father, who had been unjustly imprisoned in Paris. Her father had promised that Safie could marry Felix, but betrayed them both and forced Safie to return to Turkey with him.

- Watching the family, the monster learns about the strengths and weaknesses of mankind.

- After disposing of the remains of his second monster, Frankenstein is swept by the ocean currents to Ireland. When he lands, he is arrested for the murder of Clerval.

- Frankenstein spends two months dangerously ill in his Irish prison. He is visited by his father. The magistrate shows him kindness and eventually helps him to prove his innocence.

- News of Elizabeth's death kills Victor's father. With nothing left to lose, Victor dedicates himself to the pursuit of the monster.

Back in time

Mary Wollstonecraft Shelley was born in 1797. Her father, William Godwin, a journalist, novelist and political philosopher, is considered to have been one of the earliest anarchists. He believed that people do not require governments and laws to make them take responsibility for other people's needs. Mary's mother, Mary Wollstonecraft Godwin, who had written *A Vindication of the Rights of Woman* in 1757, was one of the first feminists. She died shortly after her daughter's birth. Mary Wollstonecraft married the poet Percy Shelley, another revolutionary thinker.

Frankenstein was published when Mary Shelley was only twenty years old. During a holiday in Switzerland with her husband and the famous poet George, Lord Byron, the three found themselves housebound by stormy weather. They decided to hold a ghost story competition, and *Frankenstein* was Mary's contribution. Mary Shelley later claimed that the story was inspired by a nightmare.

Mary Shelley, along with Percy Shelley and Byron, forms part of the 'romantic movement'.

This was a cultural reaction against the rather strict and ordered political and social situation of the time. Romanticism influenced all of the arts, including literature, music, painting and architecture. Other famous romantic poets were William Wordsworth, Samuel Taylor Coleridge and William Blake.

Romanticism valued the importance of emotions, the wildness of nature, and doing what you felt came from your deepest motivations. It was in opposition to control and restraint. The French Revolution, in which the French people rose up against their king, occurred at the same time as romantic thought was developing. Romantic thinking supported the revolutionaries.

Another boundary explored by the romantics was the limitations of human knowledge. They explored the Faust myth, in which a man, led by his own vanity and ambition, makes a pact with the devil in order to gain knowledge. They were also influenced by the Greek story of Prometheus, who stole fire from Zeus and gave it to mankind, for which his punishment was eternal suffering.

Finding out more

We recommend the following books, websites and films to gain a greater understanding of Mary Shelley and the world she lived in.

Books

- Mary Shelley, *Maurice, or The Fisher's Cot*, Viking, 1998. This children's story (suitable for age 8+) was recently discovered in a private library in Tuscany.

- Miranda Seymour, *Mary Shelley*, Picador, 2001.

- Dick Briefer (illustrator), *The Monster of Frankenstein*, Idea Men, 2007. A comic version.

- Naima Green, *Meet Frankenstein* (Famous Movie Monsters), Rosen, 2004.

- Roger Lancelyn Green, *Tales of the Greek Heroes: Retold from the Ancient Authors*, Puffin Classics, 1994. This includes the Prometheus story.

Websites

- www.bbc.co.uk/schools/gcsebitesize/
english_literature/prosefrankenstein
A useful site for studying Frankenstein,
including a summary and revision exercises.

- www.bbc.co.uk/schools/gcsebitesize/
english_literature/prosefrankenstein/oprose_
frankenstein_contrev2.shtml
Details about Mary Shelley, her life and the
historical context of *Frankenstein*.

- http://en.wikipedia.org/wiki/Romanticism
Provides a useful introduction to the romantic
period.

- www.literaryhistory.com/19thC/SHELLEYM_
Frankenstein.htm
A selective and helpful guide to links to other
Mary Shelley sites.

Films

- *Frankenstein,* Universal Pictures, 1931. Directed by James Whale.

- *Mary Shelley's Frankenstein,* UCA, 1994. Directed by Kenneth Branagh.

Food for thought

Here are some things to think about if you are reading *Frankenstein* alone, or ideas for discussion if you are reading it with friends.

In retelling *Frankenstein* we have tried to recreate, as accurately as possible, Mary Shelley's original plot and characters. We have also tried to imitate aspects of her style. Remember, however, that this is not the original work; thinking about the points below, therefore, can only help you begin to understand Mary Shelley's craft. To move forward from here, turn to the full-length version of *Frankenstein* and lose yourself in her wonderfully atmospheric writing.

Starting points

- What similarities do you see between Walton and the young Victor Frankenstein?

- What do you think about Frankenstein's desire to create new life?

- Can you find any early evidence that the monster might be good rather than evil?

- What do you notice about the relationship between Victor's moods and the scenery and weather?

- Do you ever feel that things might turn out well for Victor? Why? Why not?

- How do your feelings about the monster and Victor change as you read the story?

- How far do you agree that Victor is responsible for the monster's crimes?

- How do you feel about the ending?

- Was the story of *Frankenstein* as you had expected, or did it surprise you?

Themes

What do you think Mary Shelley is saying about the following themes in *Frankenstein*?

- nature
- ambition
- the quest for knowledge
- responsibility
- human nature

Style

Can you find paragraphs containing examples of the following?

- the use of exclamation marks
- descriptions of scenery
- the use of short sentences to create suspense
- letters to and from other characters

Look closely at how these paragraphs are written. What do you notice? Can you write a paragraph in the same style?